George the Knight

by Leon Read

Illustrated by Clare Elsom

Notes on the series

TIDDLERS are structured to provide support for newly independent readers. The stories may also be used by adults for sharing with young children.

Starting to read alone can be daunting. **TIDDLERS** help by listing the words in the book for a check before reading, and by providing visual support and repeating words and phrases. These books will both develop confidence and encourage reading and rereading for pleasure.

If you are reading this book with a child, here are a few suggestions:

1. Make reading fun! Choose a time to read when you and the child are relaxed and have time to share the story.
2. Talk about the story before you start reading. Look at the cover and the blurb. What might the story be about? Why might the child like it?
3. Look also at the list of words below - can the child tackle most of the words?
4. Encourage the child to retell the story, using the jumbled picture puzzle.
5. Give praise! Remember that small mistakes need not always be corrected.

Here is a list of the words in this story.

Common words:

a	you
are	your
is	
not	
now	

Other words:

George	knight	where
has	shield	wow
horse	sword	

George is a knight.

"You are not a knight.
Where is your sword?"

Now George has
a sword.

"You are not a knight.
Where is your shield?"

Now George has
a shield.

"You are not a knight.
Where is your horse?"

17

"Wow, George!
Now you are a knight."

Puzzle Time

Can you find these
pictures in the story?

Which pages are the pictures from?

Turn over for answers!

Answers

The pictures come from these pages:

a. pages 20 and 21

b. pages 14 and 15

c. pages 6 and 7

d. pages 16 and 17

First published in 2010 by
Franklin Watts
338 Euston Road
London
NW1 3BH

Franklin Watts Australia
Level 17/207 Kent Street
Sydney
NSW 2000

Text © Leon Read 2010
Illustration © Clare Elsom 2010

The rights of Leon Read to be
identified as the author and Clare Elsom
as the illustrator of this Work have been
asserted in accordance with the Copyright,
Designs and Patents Act, 1988.

A CIP catalogue record for this book is
available from the British Library.

ISBN 978 0 7496 9380 0 (hbk)
ISBN 978 0 7496 9392 3 (pbk)

Series Editor: Jackie Hamley
Series Advisors: Dr Hilary Minns
and Catherine Glavina
Series Designer: Peter Scoulding

Printed in China

Franklin Watts is a division of Hachette Children's Books,
an Hachette UK company. www.hachette.co.uk